T0064409

One Sohra Summer

Iadalang Pyngrope

PARTRIDGE
A Penguin Random House Company

ISBN:	Hardcover	978-1-4828-1716-4
	Softcover	978-1-4828-1715-7
	Ebook	978-1-4828-1714-0

To order additional copies of this book, contact
Partridge India
000 800 10062 62
www.partridgepublishing.com/india
orders.india@partridgepublishing.com

Dedicated to
my parents and sister

Introduction

A Sohra summer is unique. Sohra is after all, the wettest place on earth. Known to the world as Cherrapunjee, derived from a combination of the local name and the suffix '*punjee*' meaning village, Sohra conjures up images of rain-drenched mountains and cascading waterfalls. The waters feed the many streams which in turn swell the mighty rivers of Bangladesh, subsequently flooding the plains located in Khasi Hills of Meghalaya in North East India. Sohra and its surroundings provide the setting for this story. The book in essentially a fictitious account of a Khasi tribal and his family living towards the end of the eighteenth century.

What occasioned the writing of this book? Certain nuggets of information that gently nudged my imagination. A fascinating piece of information had been handed down through the generations. Great-great-grandfather Dorji (baptized 1851) was said to have narrated and passed on an interesting account of Khasis who had travelled all the way to Shilot or Sylhet (in present day Bangladesh) in the

7

closing years of the eighteenth century, to view and admire an enormous ship. It was an age prior to the advent of the British and Christianity in the Khasi Hills. As my father recounted the oft repeated lore I pictured the band of Khasis gazing at the big ship, leaving the hills for an experience they would never forget. As I would discover later, this family anecdote which came by way of oral tradition found an echo in the records of Robert Lindsay, Collector of Sylhet. In those days, the journey to Shilot was through Pandua located on the foothills. Pandua market served as a remarkable place of interaction between the hill people and the plains men. They mingled readily, selling and bartering their goods. Significantly enough, it was to this market that Krishna Chandra Pal decided to go in 1813 to preach the Gospel to the Khasis. It was the first known attempt to convert the Khasis and this he did by baptising two of them.

One Sohra Summer is an attempt to weave historical fact with fiction, in the telling of the story of Bor, a man who dared to venture out to discover new avenues. It is also the story of his daughter Bon, vulnerable yet resilient, struggling to live her life in a village somewhere near Sohra.

Principal characters in the novel

Bor	Native of Nonglum village located near Sohra
Mother of Bon	Bor's wife (it is customary to address persons as father or mother of eldest child)
Bon or Meribon Tiewsien Kerimai Rang Bok	Children of Bor
Korbar	Bor's friend
Bahrit	Bor's brother
Ban	Bor's brother-in-law
Lang Kupar	Young men of the village
Shan	Bor's nephew
Dorsing	Son of Ban
Lumbor	Bon's husband
Father and mother of Neh	Bor's neighbours

Forms of address according to custom

'Um	Short form for *Kynum* which means brother-in-law
Kha	Paternal aunt
Meisan	Mother's elder sister
Kongthei	Elder sister
Bahdeng/Bahduh	Bah is a term used to address males, 'deng' and 'duh' suffixed to qualify position or age in the family

Other terms

Sohra	Khasi name for Cherrapunjee in East Khasi Hills in the Indian state of Meghalaya, famous for being the wettest place in the world.
Shilot	Sylhet, in present day Bangladesh.
Pandua	A place on the foothills of the Khasi Hills.
Dkhar	A term used by the Khasis to refer to those non-Khasis inhabiting the plain areas.
Kwai	The practice of chewing *kwai*, a combination of areca nut, betel leaf and lime is widely prevalent among the Khasis.
Knup	Conical cane canopy worn on head as protection from rain.
Dobwai	Outer covering of areca nut tree used for wrapping foodstuff.
Iaiong	According to Khasi calendar, *Iaiong* roughly coincides with the month of April.
Jymmang	According to Khasi calendar, *Jymmang* roughly coincides with the month of May.
Nailar	According to Khasi calendar, Nailar roughly coincides with the month of August.
Duitara	Traditional string instrument.
Khathli	Fish (*Chana* spp), widely found in the Khasi Hills.
Dongmusa	Traditional torch.
Khublei Shibun	Expression of thanks or gratitude literally meaning "God bless you abundantly".

PROLOGUE

A village near Sohra. Unusual—it was the rainy season but it did not rain that day. The mists were rising from the deep gorges and the waterfalls thundered their way down the steep cliffs to dissolve in a rainbow and a smoky pool at the foot.

Many barren hills away, a little girl stood at the top of a stony projection that seemed to surge upwards away from the grassy slope that formed its base. Her hair blowing in the wind, she gazed at the plunging waterfall. Her eyes travelled from the waterfall to the hills nearby as she noticed the verdant green of the foliage covering the half—naked cliffs. Then she turned away picking her way slowly through the bare face of the huge rock. She soon reached the foot and walked towards the next hill where her village lay. Her bare feet did not feel the jagged edges of the stones. Absentmindedly she plucked a twig and started chewing it, her mind full of thoughts.

Meribon could not see the plains today, it was too cloudy. The other day she caught a glimpse when the fog lifted and the whole expanse seemed to stretch without end. It was where her father had gone. Three moons ago, her father and four other men of the village had journeyed to Shilot, the land of the *dkhar*. She wondered what they would bring back. They had carried iron, honey, lac not knowing what the response would be. Wanhat, of Pandua had given them all assurance that these items were in great demand among the plainsmen. She remembered the excitement when they left—they had never been beyond Pandua and they would be the first people from Nonglum village to venture to Shilot. She knew they were due to return any day now. She heard the grown-ups talk about it. Every day she would come to the same spot to look at the plains below. Something told her it would be different today.

She walked on. She liked to be alone, to sniff the mountain air and feel the damp fog clinging to her body. Walking slowly over the hillcrest, she spotted the cluster of huts smoking away in the distance. Suddenly, she was struck by a sense of urgency—she quickened her steps, almost running. As she approached the huts, she knew instinctively that her father had returned. There were no children playing outside, only the chickens went about their usual pecking. Quickly she ran home and entered the hut—to see her father surrounded by a large group of people, family and neighbours. He looked up and saw her, "Ah Bon; where have you been?" She stepped forward and said, "Father!"

He patted her head and she sat down next to him.

Part One

CHAPTER ONE
The Return to Nonglum

It was not one of those ordinary days, no, not a non-day. The chickens were noisier than usual and even the birds chirped louder than ever. Perhaps they sensed the excitement in the village.

Bon's mother or 'Mother of Bon' as she was popularly called in accordance with custom, had received word that the men were on their way home. In fact they had been spotted at Pandua village, situated a little further down the mountain on the other side of Nonglum.

The weary band of travellers finally made their appearance in the early afternoon. They came home to familiar smells. The fresh mountain wind and the gurgling of brook. How could they explain? It was oh! so different! There were the people, the tongas and the brisk buying and selling. Above all how could they possibly attempt to describe the big river and that huge monstrosity floating effortlessly on the waters. It was difficult to believe that beyond the waters lay other lands, other people going about their business.

They were told a white man built the ship—yes, the white man. That would be another interesting story.

In his hut, Bor looked at his five children through the smoke. "Mother of Bon", he urged his wife, "see to the fire, there is too much smoke". The woman busied herself with the logs of wood while Bon and her sisters gazed expectantly at their father. The two boys were too young to understand.

Ban, his brother-in-law, walked into the hut.

"Oh! 'Um Bor, have you arrived?"

"Yes, I have. What about you and your family, are you keeping well?"

"Yes, 'Um".

"I have such stories to tell you to keep you awake all night!"

"Really! and what is it about the land you have seen?"

Bor shook his head—"how can I describe it all? Full of wonders—there are nice things, there are bad things. Mother of Bon, is the soup ready? I'll eat the yam later."

The woman took the wooden ladle and poured the soup into an earthen bowl and placed it before him. Then she put the yam to boil in a big earthen pot. Then she went to a corner of the hut and took some betel leaves and nuts and started to peel the nut expertly with a knife. A neighbour came in. "Oh Father of Bon, you have returned! Are you well? We do want to know what stories you have to tell."

Bor replied, "Do sit down and have some *kwai*."

He took the bowl of soup in his hands, closed his eyes for a moment and inhaled deeply. Ravenous, he gulped down the soup. It was a long, long time since he had tasted soup this good.

With a torrent of words he began, words tumbling one after the other, trying, hands waving, gesticulating to somehow give shape and meaning to sights and sounds unknown to his listeners. He spoke to them of the world beyond Pandua and the journey to Shilot, Wanhat's easy banter and the discomfiture of the rest. Bor told them of his admiration for Wanhat who knew the ways of the world they had ventured into. Bor was sure they would need Wanhat's assistance for some time before they could gain enough confidence to trade on their own. There were times when Bor felt that Wanhat took on a rather condescending attitude but it had to be tolerated if they wanted to learn anything. Now and then Bor would exclaim, "Oh, my friends, my kinsmen, you cannot imagine the sense of ignorance I felt while I was there!". There were murmurs of agreement while others pointed out that the ignorance was mutual.

People in the plains were ignorant of the inhabitants of the hills too.

"Yes, my brothers, that is true", Bor said "but the world down there is different from ours. I saw the white man and the great ship that he built. Now let me tell you about that". And so, Bor continued his tale, describing the sea and the huge, gigantic ship. The waters were limitless, stretching to the horizon, the ship awe inspiring, ready to set sail. Bor had asked Wanhat many questions, wanting to know where it was bound for and who built it. He would never forget his glimpse of the white man as he sat in one of his vessels, commanding his men in the native tongue. Then there were questions about the white man. Bor did not know much but he was a keen observer and told them what he knew. One thing he understood, for all the pomposity of the rich landowners and the zamindars who seemed to have a great deal of authority, there was the power of the white man to which they had to submit. They paid revenue to the most powerful white man in the area who in turn deposited the revenue with his superiors. Bor did not seem tired at all—he continued talking animatedly, enjoying the wonder—struck expression on the faces of his listeners.

"As for the plainsmen, you know, my friends, they are not all the same. You know from experience, there are some who eat beef others who do not, some who eat pork, others who do not eat meat at all. They follow different beliefs and rituals.

"What about the white man?" Somebody asked. "What does he believe in?"

Bor was stumped—"Eh, my brother, I'm not sure, I don't really know maybe I can find out next time. They call him the Sahib though."

There were some murmurs and discussion on the matter, before Bor resumed his 'storytelling'

Bon watched her uncle seated in a corner, as he shook his head in disbelief. Meanwhile, the audience grew. There were their closest neighbours—Father of Neh and his wife, their children, and then there were also their clansmen from the other side of the hill who threw down their hoes and axes and hurried across the little hillocks as soon as they heard the news.

The tales continued—there were questions and interjections, but the narrative went on. The *kwai* was passed around and soon Bor disclosed to them that he had entered into an agreement with Wanhat of Pandua Village for the supply of various commodities, which were in great demand in the plain areas. Among them were iron, honey as well as fruits. There was general approval all around. The skeptics of course, shrugged and expressed their indifference. Bor's brother-in-law or 'Um Ban' sat in a corner smoking his pipe. Bon watched her uncle close his eyes only to open them suddenly when he heard something particularly interesting. A derisive smile soon hovered over his features as he drew on his pipe and blew out smoke to the rafters above. Bon had to admit that her father's stories were difficult to swallow. Really, the description of the white men was indeed strange. Her father certainly amazed the crowd with his story of the big boat that could float on the mighty waters that had no end. Truly, that was some story. And so it went on— the strange tales—by the light of the *dongmusa*. The audience could only say "indeed, he has done well" and privately they wondered about more immediate issues. For instance, Mother of Neh tried to imagine the taste of the dried fish Bor had brought home. She couldn't. And the rice. And the other food items.

The next morning, the village was abuzz with the very same stories. There were some who believed wholeheartedly—they consisted of families of those men who had accompanied Bor. There were others who accepted only part of the narrative and still others who declared that nothing good would come out of the whole venture. The fear of the unknown world dictated their world view. It was a world limited by age-old beliefs and compulsive insularity brought about by circumstances of history. Their kinsmen living in the villages adjoining the plains of the *dkhar* were more open to interaction with the world outside. Nonglum was situated in the hills and there was no reason for the *dkhar* to have any contact with the villages. Bor and his trading party, therefore, were regarded as crass adventurers, foolhardy enough to risk their lives. Most of all, the village was surprised to learn that Bor was already making plans for his next journey. It was an age when things moved slowly, at their own pace, when fruits and vegetables were allowed to ripen at their own will, when forests blazed furiously to make way for the year's crop and there were enough forests to burn each year. It was an age when animals had their own space, when men lived close to the soil, when few changes occurred in a man's lifetime. So it was in Nonglum, a village perched on a small plateau overlooking a sharp mountain ridge, descending into the valleys below, sloping gradually to meet the plains in the distance.

CHAPTER TWO
Circumspection

The rain drummed endlessly. It was the season after all and so typical of Sohra. The stone walls became damp and the thatch was wet and soggy. Despite the rain, people went out whenever they could. Bor wondered how many *knup* would wear out this year. The previous summer Bor used three in succession. He took his *knup* and looked at it carefully. It would still last for a month or so, he decided.

Bor walked out into the rain with the *knup* on his head. He had a lot of work to do. There were people he had to meet, markets to visit, supplies to get. The rain made things difficult for him. Yes, he had to meet Bahrit and Korbar. Their help was invaluable. His heart warmed when he thought of his younger brother Bahrit and Korbar, one of his close friends who had accompanied him to Shilot.

His next journey was scheduled for *Nailar*, just after the rainy season.

Bor reflected on the strange turn of events. He did not know what fate had in store for him but he felt positive about his future. I am lucky, he thought, to have agreed to go to Shilot with Wanhat of Pandua village. He remembered quite clearly his initial reluctance when Wanhat first broached the idea. Bor has made his acquaintance in Pandua and Wanhat had invited him to join a trading party to Shilot. At first, Bor had declined the offer, but Wanhat's persuasion soon got the better of him.

And so the days passed. The rain continued for nine days and nine nights. Finally on the tenth day, the sun broke through the clouds, shone briefly before being obscured by the thick clouds.

Bor lay awake at night thinking of new ideas, and suggestions to offer to Korbar—he liked Korbar because he spoke little and when he did it was usually to say something sensible. He thought of the other men in the village. Village elders like Thawmut voiced their opinions loudly for all to hear, "It is fine to eat the rice and fish of an alien land but one should not forget the taste of yam and tapioca of one's own backyard."

Bor took it all in his stride. His wife spoke continuously of the superior flavour of the dried fish—it was her way of telling him she approved of what he was doing. His brother, Bahrit and Korbar came over to his hut every now and then to share the memories of their journey to Shilot. They would sit around the hearth and recall their journey. Ever so often, Bor would ask his brother if he remembered a particular incident. Bahrit would nod and smile. Korbar would joke about their ignorance and Wanhat's impatience. They marvelled at his ability to grasp the language of the *dkhar*, but he assured them they would soon learn. Sometimes, Bahrit would ask Korbar, "So how do you like the rice?" and Korbar would reply, "The rice? Oh! My brother, next time, we shall bring more, we shall bring more." Then they would laugh with satisfaction. There were sober moments too as when Bahrit asked Bor "Brother, I do not understand yet, the extent of the white man's power. Who is this white man? Where did he come from?' Bor could only answer," I do not know my brother, how the plainsmen came to be ruled by the white man in spite of the fact that they are more in number probably, they were defeated in battle." "We can ask Wanhat, for he knows everything," added Korbar. Bahrit was not be satisfied easily. "Brother", he continued," do you think the white man will come to our hills, maybe even rule over us someday?"

They were quiet for sometime pondering the eventuality.

Finally Bor said, "We do not know what the future holds but you and I will be dead by then!"

Hearty laughter followed as they contemplated the first white man setting foot in villages like Nonglum, stared at by people who had never before seen a white man. Bor's thoughts drifted to the moment he saw that imperious figure sitting on a vessel. In Shilot, he had seen other white men but none possessed the aura of that particular man.

Thoughts about the white man had unsettled him momentarily and he consciously shifted his focus to his own village. There was a comforting security in being back.

Bor enjoyed the attention he received from his fellow villagers. Suddenly, he found everybody was interested in him. While he found it rather flattering, he was also keenly aware of his own ineptitude and the ignorance of his own people. There was a world of opportunities waiting if only they understood.

CHAPTER THREE
The Summons

Bor lay on his bed, staring at the rafters. He remembered how his neighbours had laughed when they saw what he was making. He explained to them that in the places he had seen, people slept on raised platforms such as the one he was making. It amused him to watch the reaction of the neighbours whenever he answered their stupid questions. It did not occur to him that he laughed at them too often for their liking.

It was a tiring day, all day he had been out in the fields trying to help. The weeds had grown so high they had completely covered the shoots. He liked to take Bon along. She was old enough to help. The other children, Kerimai, Tiewsien, Rang and Bok stayed home with their mother.

At noon, he ate the tapioca his wife had wrapped in a *dobwai*, drank some water from the spring that lay at the bottom of the valley. He had returned to work till sunset and then trekked home, his daughter following, her incessant chatter forcing him to respond.

It was late evening when he heard the summons. The drumbeats disturbed the quietness of the night.

Doong-kin-doong-kin-doong! The village crier was going about his business. Bor heard him quite clearly.

"Ka-aw! Hei! fellow-villager, fellow dweller,

Hei, you who are young, you who are old,

Hei! you who are full clad, you who are half clad,

You who draw, you who drink from the village spring,

Hei! fellow-citizens, hear and listen that tomorrow, the market day,

You shall not go to your work,

To your labour to field or jungle,

That you shall not journey to hill or valley,

That all shall come forth from their home, from their hearth,

To assemble in durbar, in surbar,

For to counsel together, for the common good, the common welfare.

Ho-ui Kiw! Ho-ui Kiw! Ho-ui Kiw!

Doong-kin-doong-kin-doong!

The drumbeats resounded through the village. There were sounds of men's voices and then the howling of dogs and all was quiet again. Some time later, the drumbeats could be heard again a short distance away and the village crier repeated his exhortation.

The next day, the sun shone brightly providing a welcome respite from the heavy showers. Bor got up at dawn, he thought he heard the pigs snorting somewhat unusually. They were just below him.

The next day, the men of the village assembled at the farthest end of the village. There was a clearing, beneath a huge ancient oak and big flat stones formed a ready platform for the men to sit on. The headman, Men-Rai, sat on one side flanked by other elders of the village. Bor sat in one corner with his brother Bahrit and Korbar. Men-Rai opened the discussion and it appeared that first and foremost the durbar would discuss the prevailing dispute between Nonglum and the neighboring village of Nongrim. The village elders spoke, one after the other, never addressing the problem directly but taking their time. Bor decided against airing his views. He listened intently but he felt his priorities were elsewhere. After considerable time had passed, the issue was addressed in a more direct manner. It was resolved after the long deliberation that a party of elders of the village would go to Nongrim to try and settle the problem.

Then, Men-Rai spoke again. "As you all know, my brothers, Bor, Korbar and Bahrit, have made a visit to faraway lands. The trip has been fairly successful, they have brought new food items with them in exchange for iron, honey and other produce of our land. I have sat with Bor, talked to him about his plans and from what I understand he is preparing for another journey soon. It is a difficult hazardous journey it is not a thing to be forced upon—who shall accompany him this time?" Men Rai paused. "It is, my brothers, a journey for those who are willing, those who have no fear for the strange and the unknown. What do you say, Oh my brothers, shall we seek the will of the gods?

"Yes we shall", the men replied with a loud voice.

And so, Thawmut, the village augurer stepped forward and sat down on the stone slab. He sat hunched, looking intently at the wooden board before him. Muttering prayers and chants he prayed for signs and omens to decide whether the journey would be favourable or not. He held an egg in his hand, muttered a final supplication and then smashed the egg against the wooden board. He studied the egg shells carefully to determine the significance of their position. The crowd peered eagerly to see the results. Simultaneously a roar arose. "It is well! It is well!"

Triumphantly Bor rose from his seat and there was silence.

"Brothers, you have seen the signs and omens, you have seen the will of the Creator, you have seen for yourself the favourable indications. What else can I say? What remains is only one question. Who shall go with me?"—he paused and looked at the crowd.

"My brother, Bahrit, is unable to join me you know his family obligations prevent him from making this journey. Korbar and my nephew, Shanbor will of course, accompany me. The load is heavy, the journey difficult but the returns are great. I will need more men. It is a long arduous journey, my brothers, a journey for the brave hearted. I say again, who will go with me?"

The *Nailar* sky was not entirely bereft of clouds. They floated casting shadows on the ground below. Birds chirped, relieved that the long wet summer had passed. Below them, the men were thinking of a related matter. The streams would be swelling with the summer waters, it would not be easy to cross the turbulent rivers. Moreover, the flood waters also seemed to cover most of the plain areas they could see from their mountain slopes. What madness! They thought, to make the journey at this time of the year!

Slowly and deliberately, Ban stood up and said, "'Um, you have led the way, you have shown us the path, you have gone beyond the hills and travelled to the distant land where no man of our village has gone before—I will come with you".

Bor was surprised, he thought his brother-in-law, Ban, did not approve of his trip, but he was pleased that he had decided to go. He nodded his head in agreement. He looked around the seated gathering. Suddenly, one of the elders of the village got up and spoke.

"I shall send my son Lang, he is young and strong, and I am sure he will prove useful, let him learn the trade. It is good for a young man to taste the hardship of the journey. What do you say, my brother?"

"Certainly, certainly", the men nodded in agreement. No one expected such a quick response from the old man. In fact he was surprised at himself. The old man was Ban's neighbour and the prospect of Ban benefiting from such a journey was not very attractive to him. Well, he could compete. He would send his son, Lang. He had no inkling of what awaited him later. His wife was livid at the casual manner in which he had volunteered to send his son on such a mad, risky enterprise, but he had spoken in the durbar and therefore he could not withdraw his offer.

After one week, Bor left with four men after the augurer declared that all was well. He was accompanied by his friend Korbar, his brother-in-law 'Um Ban, his nephew Shan and Lang. They would be joined by others at Pandua. Bor also hired porters to help carry the goods to Pandua where Wanhat would be waiting. Bor looked forward to making even more profit this time.

Chapter Four
The Call of the Plains

The rains had thickened the foliage, the paths were muddy, the stone steps were covered with moss and the going was slow. The men descended with heavy loads on their backs winding their way down the slopes. The thick jungle held all kinds of surprises, snakes slithering into the undergrowth, as the sun shone on their backs. Groups of people made their way to Pandua market, expectant of profit or simply for a good day of marketing. Bor was amiable, chatting with fellow villagers and those from other villages. Every now and then he would mention his trip to Shilot with a sense of pride. All agreed that surely Shilot offered better returns. However distance and a fear of the unknown prevented the majority of the people from undertaking such a journey.

As he rested on a large rock along with his brother-in-law Ban, Bor thoughtfully considered the strangeness of a journey with Ban. Ban had never been particularly friendly, had always been guarded and reserved since the day Bor married his sister. They were polite to each other and observed the social niceties whenever Ban visited the house. For the most part, Bor never interfered in the clan discussions that sometimes took place in his home. Bor had to admit he was surprised when 'Um Ban volunteered to join the trading party. Bor could not say no even though he was reluctant to undertake the trip with Ban. Bor wondered to himself why 'Um Ban did not send his son Dorsing instead? Perhaps, he wanted to check things out for himself before sending his son. That made sense, he thought as he resumed conversation with 'Um Ban.

Meanwhile, Korbar, constant companion and dear friend, continued to entertain Shan and the other men with anecdotes from the previous journey.His nephew Shan and the old man's son Lang, paid a great deal of attention to Korbar's slightly exaggerated stories dutifully making the right responses. Soon they reached Pandua and Wanhat eagerly welcomed them. The young men were excited and Bor found joy in their childlike amazement.

The seasons came and went. The amazement soon turned into familiarity. The repeated excursions to Shilot soon enabled Bor to speak the native tongue, making it easier for him to transact business. Bor could now manage the business on his own without depending on Wanhat. Nevertheless, Wanhat benefited greatly from Bor's new found prosperity, collecting his profit from the plainsmen Bor did business with. It was a satisfactory arrangement.

The smooth flow was sometimes interrupted. The Sahib's men were hostile at times because of the marauding parties led by neighbouring villages. The Sahib blamed the hillmen in general, not knowing which villages were responsible for the attacks. Fortunately, such episodes were temporary in nature and trade resumed after brief intervals. The trade was profitable but if there was anything Bor hated it was the weather. The heat was bearable but the dust and flies made him long for the soothing breeze of the hills.

As time passed, Ban brought his son Dorsing along. Bor valued the friendship of Korbar and the loyalty and support of Shan and Bahrit. Often there were new additions but the core group remained the same. With each successive trip, Bor made more profit and brought back enviable articles of clothing for his family. His nephew and nieces, prompted by their mother showed their respect for him in many ways. He no longer mentioned his humble beginnings, finding it unnecessary to do so. His dwelling was the largest in the village, his daughter

Bon had grown up to be a beautiful young girl, his two other daughters not as pretty, but charming in their own right. He anxiously awaited the day when his two sons would be able to join the trade. He was thankful for the manifold blessings.

CHAPTER FIVE
The Seeds of Discontent

Bon's mother hurried about her chores, grumbling to herself. "So much needs to be done, so much, but only Bon seems to have some sense of responsibility".

She placed the rice pot on the fire and continued her tirade against no one in particular. It had become a habit, to wail and moan about one's circumstances.

The rice was beginning to froth when Mother of Neh walked in. "Oh Mother of Bon! What a wonderful smell! Oh Mother of Bon!".

"Here!", replied Bon's mother from the backyard.

"Where are you?" cried Mother of Neh as she stepped out of the low door into the yard and as she saw Bon's mother.

"I say, what a wonderful smell! Is it your rice?"

"Yes, he brought a different type this time. Did you know that he also brought salt? It is so easy to use, not like our salt. I must give you some".

"Mother of Bon, you have married a worthy man—a man who feeds and clothes his family in a befitting manner—you are indeed fortunate. So, what does he barter in return? The usual, I guess."

"Oh! Whatever he can lay his hands on, mostly iron and honey, also the fruits that are in season". Bon's mother paused as she called out to her daughter to gather some pumpkins.

"Why don't you send Neh with Bon's father? I'm sure he will do well for himself. I have told you often, it is worth trying".

"You are quite right, I'll think about it, that is, if Neh's father does not object".

"Why should he?" questioned Bon's mother indignantly. "He will be earning by the sweat of his brow".

Neh's mother was silent. The arguments she had with her husband were fresh in her memory. She remembered one night when she had meekly suggested that perhaps—well, perhaps—it might be better for Neh to join the trading party than to work with the ironsmith of the adjoining village. Her husband had become furious and shouted that no son of his would work with Bor and their family. Neh's mother had widened her eyes in astonishment and asked, "But why?" The man had become enraged, his eyes livid—"Because I say so!" She protested timidly, "But . . . ."

"Will you be quiet, woman?" he turned his back to her, closed his eyes and soon he was snoring noisily.

Neh's mother thought deeply. It was true that Bor's family seemed very prosperous. The neighbours spoke of brass pots and pans and copper utensils kept in a huge wooden chest. Bon had unwittingly told some friends at the village stream that her father had brought some gorgeous coral beads the last time he came home. Her mother was waiting for a suitable occasion to display them. Many thoughts floated in her mind. Through the haze she could see Bon's mother saying something, eyes moving.

"Have you become deaf woman ?" Bon's mother paused and looked into her eyes. "You have not eaten *Kwai*, have you forgotten ? The curious neighbour avoided the piercing gaze and glanced at the open doorway through which she could see Bon returning.

"I was just thinking about what you said, you know about Neh"

"Oh yes; as I said, it is better to send him with the father of my children", and she continued with a tinge of pride, "look at us, how poor we were, but now, we can walk in the village with our heads held high.

"Yes, indeed", said Mother of Neh and then she turned to speak to Bon, "Bon, my child how are you ?

How gracious and pretty she has become ? Isn't it so, Mother of Bon ?

And the conversation continued. Bon's mother took out some more betel-leaf, rubbed some lime and offered it to the visitor along with a piece of chopped betel nut. They talked about the skirmishes with the neighbouring village of Nongrim. The problem was becoming more acute and an air of restlessness pervaded the village.

The discontent was evident at the village durbars. One man had raised his voice loudly to make his point.

"Well, what about those who have forgotten their responsibilities for the village—those who choose to earn great wealth in faraway lands?"

The men had sulked in silence. For most of them Shilot represented a vague notion of an endless expanse of shimmering water during the monsoon. The *dkhar*, they knew spoke in a tongue they did not understand, dressed differently and had strange ways. Surely it was enough to do business at Pandua market where many tribesmen were present, why be too ambitious?.

There were disgruntled murmurs in the durbar. Everybody knew it would always be the same. The truth was no one dared open his mouth when Bor was present in the durbar. How could any body possibly go against a man who walked the village as if he owned each cobbled path, each hill and valley. There was one thing they didn't mind, though, his hookah, which he passed around during a dorbar, much to the delight of the menfolk.

CHAPTER SIX
A Man Like Us

The sun broke through the clouds, peered at humanity below and saw a long trail of men making their way up the mountainous cliffs with heavy loads on their backs. The cascading waterfalls jumped and skipped past them, lovingly caressing the rounded rocks dotting the mountain stream.

Bor walked across the stream carefully stepping on the slippery stones. As he neared the middle, the water covered his ankles and he was wading in knee deep water. He was on the other side soon enough but not without an appendage. As he started to climb the slope he noticed a leech clinging to his leg. He gave it a sudden slap with the palm of his hands and it fell off. He resumed his journey.

It was a big party this time—twelve men from different villages. He turned to look at his nephew Shan who was busy talking with Lang. They were animatedly discussing the journey they had made. Going up the slope he mused over what had happened. Five years ago, he had left for Shilot for the first time. It was not a long time but long enough for the village to acknowledge the utility of such a journey. But, in some way, he had to admit that there was a distance between him and his fellow villagers. His thoughts turned to his wife. It was indeed difficult for her. She had to take care of the house and all the daily requirements—come to think of it—he had been away for a long time. He would spend more time with his sons this time. They were growing up and he needed to be there. Bahdeng and Bahduh were full of promise. He looked forward to the day when they would be able to join him.

The sun was going down but the evening was rather warm. The sweat trickled down his brow. There seemed to be a clearing ahead and Bor walked towards it wiping the sweat with the palm of his hand. As he waited for the others, his thoughts turned to the last conversation he had with Wanhat.

"Remember Bor, iron is one thing, limestone another" Wanhat had said.

He admired Wanhat, yes, he admired that man for his business acumen and to have talked to a white man was no small thing—no petty thing. The Sahib had expressed a great deal of interest in limestone trade. Wanhat had arranged a meeting between the Sahib and the chiefs who would authorise the extracting of limestone.

Eating the jackfruit he carried, he chuckled to himself as he recalled the white man's face as the canoe approach the rapids. The Sahib had expressed his wish to inspect the limestone mountain. Bor could see the white man's face when the canoe narrowly missed the huge rocks as it swirled through the waters. Bor remembered each feature of that well-known face. The Sahib was the repository of power and even though they understood little of the extent of his authority, yet they knew he represented some powerful entity that made its presence felt in so many ways. But on that canoe ride, when fear and apprehension clouded the Sahib's face for a fleeting moment, Bor recalled, thinking, 'why! he is a man like us!.

Bor ate the jackfruit slowly as he watched Shan and Lang make their way up the slope. Bor smiled, he envied their enthusiasm. Behind them, Korbar and 'Um Ban followed. The sun began to set and the men hoisted their loads as they climbed the slope. Above them on a small rock, a wild boar looked at them, snorted angrily and ran off.

Part Two

CHAPTER ONE
Confutation

People began to refer to him as Bor Shilot to differentiate between the many Bors in the village. He rather liked it.

It was a fine morning and Bor walked out of his hut surveying the landscape with a sense of satisfaction. He was determined to go to his village, Mawsan the following week. His sister would be glad to see him and he also looked forward to meeting his nephew again. Shan had indeed been a great help. He was glad his sister had sent him.

Bor thought of Rupa, his niece. She was beautiful with dark lustrous hair and a complexion that set it off beautifully. This time he had a special gift for her. He could have sent it through Shan but he wanted to give it to her personally and to watch her reaction. He was sure she would be delighted.

"Bon, Bon!" he called out "have you received any news from your Kha?

"No, father, but she left word that she would like to meet you".

"Next week you will go with me, my daughter, Rupa would like to see you, wouldn't she?" Bon turned abruptly and entered the hut. Bon's mother walked into the courtyard and said, "Bon has been sulking. This morning she left the vegetables boiling—the stew had to be given to the pigs and I had to cook all over again. I wonder why she is behaving in this manner."

Bor simply shrugged and then sitting near the doorway he said to his wife, "I was thinking of taking her to Pandua market next week, would you also like to go?"

"Of course, Father of Bon, there are so many things I would like to get from the market. What about your next journey? When do you intend to leave?"

"Soon enough, soon enough! But I still need more time. Didn't I tell you, this trip is important because I will not be dealing only in the usual commodities? Moreover, Wanhat has asked me to help manage the limestone business. Even if I explained all the details, you would not understand, woman!"

"Indeed, I wouldn't! I have never been beyond Pandua, how can I ever dream of the world you talk about!" Changing the subject, she asked him, "Who will go with you on your next trip?"

"Well—the same people, Bahrit, 'Um Ban and Dorsing, my nephew Shan and Lang. Korbar, of course, will not join us this time, he has all those family rituals to attend to—but I need more men. I think there will be many from my village.

"Yes, yes", agreed his wife "I am sure there will be many men from Mawsan."

"Bahdeng! Bahduh!" she called her sons, but there was no response. Mumbling to herself she got up and went into the hut, grumbling all the while. Where were the children she wondered!

It had become a habit with her. It was part of life, part of existence itself. If it was hot, one should grumble about the heat, if it was cold one should again express a dislike for the cold. She had a nagging feeling that if she expressed a sense of satisfaction with her condition, she would invite the wrath of the Creator and her world would turn topsy-turvy. Most of all, the neighbours liked the tone of the conversation if she complained about things in general. It made them feel she was one of them.

She heard Bor's voice outside. He was enquiring whether she was ready with the food. He was in a hurry to go out. Soon, she was busy with the serving of food. He was a voracious eater and she enjoyed watching him as he ate.

Shortly after, he left the house. Bor had changed in appearance. His bearing was erect, there was firmness in every step and when he passed by, no one ignored him. They would speak to him with respect and this amused him greatly. He could not help but notice that the elders of the village paid great attention to him in the durbar.

He walked down the stone steps to the house of Thawmut. There were a few things he wanted to discuss. As he turned a corner he suddenly saw his aunt at the bottom of the steps. He did not want to meet her but there was no way he could turn back. She had seen him already. He continued down the steps and greeted her, "Meisan, how are you?"

He did not expect a civil reply but there were two women along with her so it was impossible for him not to talk to her. The old woman looked at him and said, "My son, life has not changed much for me. Ever since you deprived me of my rightful share, I have gone through much suffering. I am only a poor, destitute old woman, how can I impose my will on those who are rich and wealthy? No one listens to me now that my brother is no more. You have done well for yourself, the village holds you in great honour but you have failed your own relatives."

Bor could feel the blood rush to his face, what right had she to accuse him? Completely astounded, he murmured some excuses, tried to blabber something, but she did not listen. She turned to her companion and exclaimed, 'Wow! Do you have any idea how pride has made him forget his obligations to his own clan, to poor relatives like me? When he was poor, he was generous with the little he had, now that he is rich, you will rarely see him visiting his less fortunate clansmen. He does not want to part with his money."

Knowing he could not match her tirade, Bor said,

"You may say whatever you want but the fact is, my wealth is my own doing, it is the result of back-breaking labour and if you expect me to give away my hard-earned possessions to people who spend their days in idleness then you are mistaken."

He went down the steps in a huff, determined to avoid her at all costs in future. But she was not finished. She shouted,

"Can you deny it? You used what was mine to get capital for your trade and I trusted you but now you pretend to have forgotten everything."

Bor continued his way down the steps cursing under his breath but he could still hear her proclaim a final damning.

The cry came to him clearly, borne by the wind; it sent shivers up his spine though outwardly he appeared unmoved. The old woman's voice, trembling in anger, reached his ears,

"Because you have committed a crime and you have disregarded the half-clad and the poor, may you be devoured by the tiger, may you be struck by the thunder and may the pestilence strike you!"

Bor felt his knees go weak. Had the essence of his being left him?

CHAPTER TWO
The Augury

It was Springtime. The days passed by and when he felt the time was right, Bor sent word to his brother Bahrit, Korbar, 'Um Ban and the others to prepare for the journey. He was sure there would be another addition to the party, Kupar—now there was a fine youngman!—he had expressed a liking for Bon and Bor was pleased at the prospect. But there were things that disturbed him; the village folk did not stop by to chat as often. Well, they could do what they liked. He was busy after all, his mind churning with the thought of the approaching journey.

Perhaps it all started with the copper and the brass utensils. The nagging thought could not be dismissed entirely. Or was it the fine clothes his wife had been wearing of late. Most of the village folk wore nothing but coarse cotton. He could not say exactly what triggered the envious looks. Had he not brought some semblance of prosperity to his village? Had he not opened their eyes to the world beyond? What a pity, he thought to himself they do not know the world beyond Pandua market.

His thoughts turned to his sons, Rang and Bok. The following year would see them join the trading party. Rang or Bahdeng as he was called at home would be old enough to withstand the hazards of the journey. A man had to be tough, willing to use his hands if necessary to keep away all kinds of predators. He also realised that taking them along with him would mean extra work for his wife and daughters.

It was a crucial day for him. He thought he would take a short nap before leaving for the durbar but he couldn't sleep. He opened his eyes wide. How could a man sleep when such an important issue was at stake? The village would assemble to discuss the next journey because of the new implications. It would not be trade in the usual goods, but it involved limestone as well and that meant it included other villages too. He rose from his bed and went out, shouting as he went, "Mother of Bon, I am going!"

As Bor walked past the huts he could see the womenfolk look at him. Gossip! he thought disgustingly—there was nothing more damaging than malicious gossip and that woman—Mother of Neh was responsible. Angrily he spat out the *kwai* he had been chewing. Women!

Minutes later, Bor sat among his fellow villagers. Men-Rai started the discussion with references to the problems encountered by the people of Nonglum in relation to the surrounding villages. There were feuds and clashes and Men-Rai asked for suggestions to work out an amicable settlement. Men spoke one at a time, offering suggestions. Bor was quiet. Ever since he had opted for the Shilot trade he had lost contact with things happening back home so he dared not open his mouth. His turn would come later. At last, they resolved on a plan of action. Bor was thinking of other things. He paid little attention to the goings-on. Then he heard Men-Rai's voice, "Now, my brothers let us talk about the Shilot trade." He talked at length about the benefits of Bor's trading venture. He then referred to the expanding nature of the trade and the importance of consulting other villages.

The men were quiet, the afternoon was sultry— the birds were silent—perhaps they found the day a little hot. Bor could sense hostility—it was there somewhere among the gathering. He scanned the faces but could see nothing.

It eventually transpired that Korbar would not be able to make it this time. Men-Rai informed his audience that Korbar had some family obligations which prevented him from embarking on a journey of any sort.

"My brothers, the old and the young, who will take Korbar's place? Father of Bon, do you know of any relative of yours willing to go?"

Bor quickly replied, "I already have some relatives in the trading party so I have no objection if anyone else would like to join us."

And then Men-Rai spoke again,

"So my brothers, you have heard the plain-speak of the people involved, so is there anyone ready to join them?" He looked around at the men seated around him.

An old man stood up, "I am not as strong as I used to be and I have no strength to climb hills and descend steep valleys. But I will send my son Kupar. You all know him, he is a fine obedient young lad and I know that he will be an asset to the group."

There were murmurs all around. Kupar was not in the durbar but everyone knew they could take his father's word. The old man was well respected and his son was equally well loved.

The old man continued, "I want him to see how other people live and die, how they buy and sell, if their hopes and fears are like ours—so he may return and tell me wonderful stories as we sit around the fireplace at night."

There were grunts of approval. Bor smiled, he liked the old man. He went home feeling pleased with himself.

The next few days were spent in a flurry of activity. There were stores to be collected and Bor regretted the fact that Korbar would not be able to accompany them. He was such a great help. Anyway, he reasoned, there was Bahrit, 'Um Ban, Dorsing, Shan, and of course Kupar, who was the new addition.

Finally, the day arrived. Bor was busy checking the loads to be carried. It was a cloudy day and Bor anxiously wrapped the precious commodities with animal hide to protect them from rain.

His brother-in-law arrived with Thawmut the village augurer. Soon Bor, 'Um Ban and Thawmut sat in front of the hut—intent on the task before them. As they sat concentrating on the augurer's task, huge drops of rain fell on the ground. Thawmut continued his incantation, face wrinkled in concentration. Suddenly, the rain came in a hesitant spatter at first and then a steady flow. Thawmut collected his articles of divination and hurriedly scuttled to a corner sheltered by a huge square overhanging thatch. 'Um-Ban followed him as Thawmut said loudly,

"Just as well, Bor's hut is large." 'Um Ban muttered a reply. Meanwhile Bor hurriedly collected the fruit left outside to dry in the sun. There were the animal skins too.

As he went inside the hut, he called out,

"Old man-Thawmut, go ahead! I am coming in a moment".

"As you say!" replied Thawmut.

Thawmut held an egg in his hand as he muttered an incantation to ask for Divine Revelation. Finally, he smashed an egg against the board. His face clouded—clearly the egg had revealed bad omens.

Inside the hut, Bor shouted, his voice almost drowned by the sound of the rain,

"How goes it, 'Um?"

Thawmut was about to open his mouth but 'Um Ban quickly answered,

"It is fine, 'Um."

Thawmut started to protest but he was silenced by the look on Ban's face. And then, to Thawmut, Ban said,

"It is not all bad, is it, my elder brother?"

"No, it is not"—Thawmut said slowly—but he shook his head and shrugged his shoulders.

Outside the torrent continued to startle the dust until there were no dry patches left. Soon water dropped from the roof's edges and formed little dents on the earth.

Thawmut went on looking intently at the egg shells.

"This is not to be ignored—this is a sign from the gods. Bor! Will you come here for a moment!"

The rain poured, as if beating a thousand drums and Ban pointed to his ears indicating that even he could not hear what Thawmut said. The water dripped around them but they were not wet. Bor seemed to be busy; he did not come out of the hut.

Both of them sat there looking at the wooden board before them and then at the rain-soaked earth.

They sat there while the showers decreased in intensity and then Thawmut cried out once again,

"Oh Bor! Do come and see for yourself!"

"Yes I will!" came the reply.

Inside the hut, Bor was trying to decide how to carry the cowries. There were so many, he would have to ask the young men to help him. There were things to barter, but cowries were so convenient except when there were too many sometimes.

Again, he heard Thawmut calling him. Why couldn't they settle it themselves, he thought. He was sure the signs would be favourable. In all these years, not once had the gods been unkind to him, there was no reason why the results would show otherwise this time.

The rain became a drizzle and Thawmut emerged from the overhanging thatch.

"Oh Bor, Bor! The rain has stopped. I shall go home because I am in a hurry but do see for yourself the revelation of the gods. Ban will tell you. It is not good but not all bad either! It is up to you!"

As soon as Thawmut left, 'Um Ban scooped up the eggshells with a deft movement of his right hand. Minutes later, Bor stepped out and said, "What, 'Um, it is all right, is it not?"

"Oh yes, 'Um, nothing to worry about", 'Um Ban replied as he took some water from the wooden barrel outside and splashed some of it on his feet.

CHAPTER THREE
Shadow of the Serpent

Bon's mother wrapped the tapioca carefully in the *dobwai*. She was sure it would last. God alone knows how they survived the journey. She woke up when the cock crowed and it took a moment or two for her to remember with a start that the men were leaving that day.

Bon watched her father getting ready. Along with her brothers she helped with the bundles of provisions the men were to carry to far-away lands. She was proud of her father but she was big enough to understand that all was not well. At the village stream the women spoke of many things. They spoke of sudden wealth, of wealth that comes like a flash flood, of men who ignore the opinions of those who have seen the sun and the moon long before they were born.

She could see Kupar approaching.

'Kongthei', there is Bah Kupar!' said her brother excitedly.

"I know, Bahdeng, you don't have to shout." She replied, a trifle embarassed.

Bahduh the youngest, looked at her pointedly and remarked,

"You're blushing!"

"Be quiet Bahduh", she admonished him.

Bahdeng was staring at the group of men hoisting the loads onto their shoulders. "Kongthei", he said longingly, "when will father allow me to go with him?"

"I do not know Bahdeng, perhaps next year . . ."

Kupar walked down the path along with a group of friends. They had come to see him off. As he neared the banyan tree where Bon stood with her brothers, he raised his hand and waved. Little did she know that it would be the last time. As the party disappeared from sight, she took another path which led to her favourite spot, a vantage point from where she could see the surrounding hills.

Her brothers scampered ahead of her knowing exactly what she intended. Soon they reached the spot and sat, waiting for the men to be visible.

On the other side, the gorges were steep, there were flowers suspended here and there, against a background of green. Some flashed their loud colours, some barely made their presence felt in hues that merged with their background. Bon listened to the sound of the water but it was not very audible.

Then she saw them, seven figures walking carrying their heavy loads on their backs. They were too far away to see her but she called out a greeting anyway.

"Go in peace", she said. She knew they would be joined by others from neighbouring villages. Her heart filled with sadness because it would be a long time before they returned.

She decided to visit Rimai, her friend later in the evening. It would be wonderful to catch up with the latest gossip.

That evening as Bon sat in Rimai's hut, animatedly discussing the Shilot trip, her father and Wanhat were engaged in serious talk about the possibility of abandoning all thought of proceeding further. Wanhat informed them that it was dangerous to proceed beyond Pandua as the plainsmen were hostile to the Khasis, on account of the murder of one of them by the tribesmen. It appeared that the white man in command had come to know of the incident and had stationed soldiers to guard the foothills. Wanhat advised the trading party to stay in Pandua till the situation improved. Bor reluctantly agreed. He knew that he could get a better price for his products in Shilot, now, that things had taken an unexpected turn, he would have to consult the others. It irritated him somewhat to admit that their journey would take longer than usual and that they would not be able to return home before summer.

A week after, Wanhat decided that risky though it still was, there was no harm in trying. They ventured, cautiously, anxious not to arouse suspicion even though they carried their weapons with them. Wanhat, knew the tongue of the plainsmen as did Bor, and together they succeeded in convincing the soldiers that they were tradesmen and not marauders. Finally, they reached Shilot and commenced their business. While they were in Shilot, the summer clouds gathered in the sky, the rains were early that year.

It was a long, long summer. Bon was surprised, even slightly worried by the fact that her father had not returned. Time and again, she watched the plains fill up with water and she wondered where the men were and how they survived the fury of nature. She found it difficult to understand how her father and the other men carried out their business in the face of such a situation. She would often voice her thoughts to her mother who would promptly laugh; telling her there was absolutely no need to understand everything under the sun.

She found some comfort in Rimai, her friend who listened patiently, offering some comments from time to time, not that she visited her friend often. It was impossible to do so because of the heavy rain.

As the days passed her restlessness grew. She felt lonely and she missed Kupar. What tales he would recount when he returned! It would certainly be exciting.

One morning she walked as usual to her favourite spot, overlooking the hill slopes and the surrounding valleys. It was a place she loved. Countless times she had trudged towards this place to spend hours in thinking of her loved ones. The orange butterflies flitted from flower to shrub. A hawk flew high overhead scouring the earth below. Reaching the top, she sat down. There was a butterfly close to her foot, quivering gently. Flexing her toes she wondered what it would be like to wear shoes. Her father had told her that in the plains the rich wore coverings for their feet. Absentmindedly, she plucked some leaves from a shrub nearby. What would her father bring her this time? She simply could not wait for the right occasion, she wanted to show off the new clothes and the coral beads her father brought her last year. Rimai's wedding would be a good opportunity. And Kupar, would Kupar be there to see her?

On a mountain side, miles away, a band of weary travellers gathered round the limp figure of Kupar. Bor put his hand on Kupar's chest. He shook his head—'he is not yet gone but his condition is getting worse'. Shan sighed, "We have done our best to try and get the venom out. Is there anything else we can do? God is witness to our efforts."

The others stood silently. Why did it happen? The trip had been fairly successful after the initial hurdles. The profits were considerable, in fact Wanhat was so pleased with Bor that he had asked Bor to stay on at Pandua to help him.

Bor turned his face away. His heart was heavy. Oh Kupar! You were so strong and full of promise! He recalled the excitement in the young man's eyes. It was his first trip to the land of the *dkhar*. Kupar and Shan had the energy and spontaneity of youth. Full of humour, they laughed and conversed all the way, their witticisms entertaining the older men who were pre-occupied, most of the time, with their own thoughts. 'Um Ban remarked "It must have been a deadly snake". After a pause, he continued, "we should not move him, who knows, his spirit and strength may return."

Bor was lost in his own thoughts. Kupar's family, his parents had trusted him with their only son. What explanation could he give them!

They left him in the same place half hoping that he would emerge from his coma. The nights were rather chilly even though the days were quite hot. They had made a makeshift shelter out of dried branches and leaves and the men were in a pensive mood. It was still a long way home. The nearest village was Nongrit. There were relatives in that village. Surely, they would render some help. Perhaps some medicine man in the village would provide a remedy. Bor stared into the fire, at the burning embers, thinking about the next course of action. The night resounded with the eerie howl of foxes. As he sat beside the fire, he thought he saw a pair of eyes looking at him from the undergrowth. Could be a leopard, he thought, but the eyes disappeared after some time.

The next morning, 'Um Ban echoed his thoughts,

"Oh 'Um! Today it is better that we proceed to Nongrit with Kupar. What do you say?"

"Certainly, that is the best way".

Bor was confused. His mind was in a quandary. What would Kupar's parents say? They made a bamboo bier. Silently, they worked. Unspoken words speaking louder than what they actually said to each other. Their progress was slow, a new burden adding to the already existing ones. The men walked quietly along the mountain path, only their heavy sighs were audible at intervals. 'Um Ban started lamenting out loud.

"Oh why have you punished us so? Have we done any wrong to man that you should cause this to happen, this young man, innocent and helpless".

"Keep silent", Bor cried out in anger, "You speak as if he is dead".

'Um Ban kept quiet, sullenly looking at Bor. They reached Nongrit but the first hut by the roadside was quiet. They have gone out to the fields, they thought. When they reached the centre of the village and realised that it was deserted they were alarmed. There was no sign of life. Finally, Bor called out loudly, "Is there anybody there?" A chicken flapped its wings, startled "Where have they all gone?" Shan wondered. There were no flickering lights. Bor looked around, "what could be the reason? Is there anybody there?" he again repeated.

Shan who was holding up the sick man along with Dorsing said. "I'm too tired—I'm going to sit right here". With that he and Dorsing lowered the sick man and sat beside him, wiping the sweat off their brows.

Meanwhile, Bor with *dongmusa* in hand climbed up the stone steps to one of the huts. After some time he reappeared "Nobody there", he repeated. "Should we go on farther?" 'Um Ban asked. "Perhaps there are people on the other side".

Bor answered, "I think we should stay here for the night. We are tired and it is proper that we should take rest. What a pity! I thought we could get some help for Kupar. Shan! How is he?"

Shan shook his head, "His condition is the same, uncle."

Bor sighed, "Well so what do we do now?" We have done all we could. You get some sleep. I will keep watch."

Chapter Four
Lament for the Dead

Bon lay awake, listening to the owl hooting. She could not sleep but she could hear her sister's breathing. Her mother was snoring noisily, keeping to a strange kind of rhythm with the hooting of the owl. Bon tossed left and right and finally in the early hours she fell asleep.

When she woke up she was in a bad mood, scolding her younger brothers for no reason at all. They stared at her but withheld their complaints. The fire was glowing and she put the yam to boil. She walked out into the backyard and noticed that she had forgotten to bring in the fruit she had kept to dry. Now they were wet and soggy with the morning mist. She looked out to the distance and her eyes focused unconsciously on a tree at the far end of the hill on her left. To her amazement the tree began to sway a little. Bon blinked and looked again—yes, the tree was slowly, very slowly, leaning towards one side. But there was no breeze, no wind, she said to herself. And then quite determinedly, almost decisively the tree came crashing down hitting the ground with a loud thud, its branches shuddering before lying quite still.

Far away, in a village called Nongrit a group of men stood around Kupar. They knew the life had gone out of him. Shan broke into tears while Bor turned away from them and stood leaning against a tree. Kupar's parents—what would they say. And his daughter, the poor girl had loved him so. There would be no comforting her. His thoughts were rudely shattered by 'Um Ban's voice.

"What has brought about this unfortunate event? Is it some taboo we have broken?"

Bor bowed his head, burdened with grief; he remained speechless. Suddenly, they heard footsteps and soon a man appeared on the edge of the hill.

"Oh my brothers" he cried out "Pray what are you doing here? 'Um Ban replied—"We have returned from a long journey but where is everybody? We spent the night here because the village seemed so quiet."

"Oh didn't you know? The pestilence has wiped out many families. So many people have died; in fact, I have lost count. Almost everyday we buried people. I saw your fire in the night so I came over to see."

"Then we have a problem". Bor said, "'Um what shall we do with the dead body? It is still far from our village. I thought we could get some help here but it seems they have all fled the place."

The stranger started when he heard mention of a dead body.

"Whose dead body?"

"It's a long story". Bor wearily answered. It was a subject he was not eager to elaborate. Bor shouted to the others,

"Hei Shan! Dorsing! Do come here and help decide what we should do."

After lengthy deliberation they decided to bury Kupar in Nongrit and proceed with their journey. The presence of the pestilence necessitated such an unusual step. It was decided that they return to Nonglum and inform the relatives. At some later date, all the rites and ceremonies of cremation would then be observed. Of course, they would have to return to the spot for the body. They had marked it with a stone. Bor was sure they would have no trouble finding it.

Alas! it was not so simple. The news of Kupar's death paralysed the whole village. They wanted to know all the details. 'Um Ban gleefully obliged each time as he narrated the circumstances leading to Kupar's death. Bor was too full of grief to talk. In some way, he felt responsible and this made him hold back his real emotions except to declare once in a while,

"You know, we did everything we could".

Ban saw the episode as a God-given opportunity to knock his brother-in-law off the pedestal he had been placed. He would say to scores of listeners, "Yes, we tried to revive him but there were only the two of them when the snake bit him so one cannot say what really happened. Only God the Creator knows the truth".

The hidden implications were not lost on the listeners and the gossip began. Bor felt the accusing glances as he went about his work. But there were faces he simply could not forget. The pain was evident in the eyes of Kupar's aged parents, when they heard of their son's death. Moreover, the grief he could clearly see in Bon was unspeakable. It overwhelmed her completely as the tears streamed down her face and her voice choked with intense sorrow. For weeks she went about her household chores without talking, not even the clothes he brought her gave her any joy.

At last, they received news that people were returning to their pestilence-ravaged villages. The pestilence had passed. Kupar's family decided it was time to complete the rites for the cremation of their son. His uncles, both maternal and paternal, were sent to Nongrit to bring the body or what was left of it to Nonglum for proper cremation.

When the men arrived, it was a heartbreaking scene. Kupar's mother wailed, her voice filling the air as she cried:

> "Oh my son, why have you left your
> Mother and father without a word!
> Why have you fled suddenly, before your time!
> Who will look after field and fowl?
> Who will look after the sowing and the reaping?
> Who will fend us from the ill-meaning stranger?
> Tell me, answer me my morning star!
> My dearest son, so dear to my heart!"

Her cries rent the air and Bor sat in a corner, his head bowed.

CHAPTER FIVE
Revelry Among The Living

Kupar's unexpected demise affected the general mood of the village. But with his cremation there was a sense of finality that nothing more could be done. Winter came and went. The cycle of life and death in man finding resonance in nature. It was soon time to celebrate. Rimai and Lang were getting married. Rimai's mother was heard boasting of her daughter's good fortune. She was sure her future son-in-law showed a certain aptitude for the Shilot trade. When she expressed this sentiment during one of her visits to a neighbour's house she was reminded rather sardonically of Kupar's fate. She was advised to contain her boasting. It would only serve to attract the wrath of the Creator.

The day of the wedding soon dawned. There was great activity all around. The village throbbed with life. Wafts of smoke declared all around that the cooking was in full swing. It was said that some special rice had been acquired for the purpose. Boiled pork soup and other delicacies conjured visions of a lavish feast. There would be roast pork to be carved by sharp knives and sumptuously eaten on plantain leaves. Liquor would of course add to the royal spread.

Across the other side of the village, in Bor's house, Bon looked at her mother as she carefully took out the fine clothes from the wooden trunk.

"Oh! mother, they look beautiful don't they!"

"Yes, my daughter, they would have looked beautiful on you but you refuse to go so what can I do?"

"Mother! let's not talk about it! You know how I feel."

"My daughter, there are other young men and if you would go with your sisters to the wedding you would surely meet someone."

Bon was tired of the subject and said, "Mother, you had better get dressed quickly or you will be left behind".

Her sister Kerimai was fastening the knots on her shoulders. She twirled her long thick hair in her palm and twisted it into a thick knot at the top of her head. "Kongthei", she said, "how do I look"?

Before Bon could answer, Tiewsien snapped, "you look fine—you always do, now pass me the comb". Kerimai tossed the bamboo comb and Tiewsien ran the fine comb through her hair, and in a softer voice pleaded,

"Kongthei, please, do come with us".

"You, too, harping on the same thing—I don't feel like going and that's that".

Tiewsien cast her a glance and when she saw how determined Bon was, she said

"Well, as you wish, we'll have more gold to wear, won't we Mother?"

The mother smiled, a smug look on her face.

Just then, Neh's mother called out,

"Mother of Bon! Oh Mother of Bon! Are you ready?"

"Yes, Mother of Neh, do come in!"

The curious neighbour stepped into the hut and saw them in their finery. Her mouth opened wide, she stared at them without any attempt to hide her amazement. She stood there gazing at clothes, the likes of which she had never seen before.

"Really, Mother of Bon, your daughters look absolutely stunning, why, you look like a young girl yourself, and you are positively glowing."

"Oh really!" she blushed, pleased with the compliments, "Do hurry children!"

Neh's mother continued to inspect the clothes. Her eyes rested on the fine silk tassels at the bottom, travelled upwards to the jewellery, the huge coral beads that must have cost a fortune, the gold earring, looped round the ears and suddenly she became aware of her own plain, dull-looking attire. At last she could not resist commenting,

"I hope you don't mind my asking but are these coral beads from Shilot?"

"Oh, of course, where do you suppose we got them from? Kerimai! Tiewsien! let us go."

Bon watched them leave. Her heart ached with longing for Kupar.

The bride and bridegroom looked resplendent. Prior to the wedding day, both sides had met and satisfied themselves that there was no taboo, no obstruction whatsoever to the uniting in marriage of both Lang and Rimai.

It was, therefore, with a sense of great joy that they welcomed the bridegroom's party with *kwai* and then escorted Lang and his relatives to Rimai's house for the ceremony. Lang was seated next to Rimai as an old man carefully mingled the fermented liquor of both sides together. The ceremony continued until the chanting began in earnest.

> "Hei, Oh God, Creator of all, . . .
> thou shall know, thou shall hear,
> that they are married this day,
> bless them that they may prosper and multiply,

in their hut in their hearth

that they may increase, that they

may be well . . ." and so it went on and on

until finally some liquor was poured on the

ground accompanied by a

suitable invocation to the Creator and

ancestors.

There was a festive air in the village. Nonglum was full of clansmen of the bride from far-off villages. All except Kupar's family attended the feast.

In the evening, people returned to their homes animatedly discussing the food, the heavy jewellery Bon's mother flaunted, putting even the bride to shame. There was indeed a general disapproval at the vulgar display of wealth. The sighs and murmurs gave way to hearty laughter echoing in the stillness of the night. As the people wound their way up and down the village paths their torches flickered, dotting the dark landscape.

Gradually, the sound of the revellers could no longer be heard. The moon emerged from the thick clouds and cast its light on the earth. The stillness was shattered by the howling of foxes in the jungle nearby. Soon the dogs joined the chorus and a cacophony ensued.

CHAPTER SIX
Confrontation

Dorsing did not like it one bit. What an argument they had had! His father and uncle were at loggerheads—never had he detected so much rage in his father's voice. It was true they had drunk a little too much. The liquor was of the finest quality, who could blame them? But such harsh words—when his mother heard about it, she had tried to calm him down. She had said,

"Father of Dorsing, we owe a lot to them. You should have exercised some restraint."

But he would not listen. Dorsing could not imagine that such a display of hostility between his father and uncle was possible. Maybe, he thought to himself, they would forgive and forget, Dorsing had heard his father complain of his uncle's highhandedness but he never imagined it would come to this.

Dorsing thought about how it all started. The men had lit a fire outside in the evening. True, winter had passed but the evenings were chilly. Men-Rai the village headman had asked him,

"Well son, will you be going with your father this time?"

"Yes, Grandpa", he replied.

"And when do you plan to go?"

"I don't really know, probably the end of *Jymmang*."

Bor, who was also present, interrupted,

"No, no, who said so? We will go earlier. As soon as the new moon comes up we will leave. The time is right and Wanhat will be expecting us."

"But, uncle, I heard father say that we should wait till the end of *Jymmang*."

Bor had turned to him angrily and said,

"Your father! what does your father know? Was it not I who started all this trade in the first place. Look at your family. Two years ago, you did not know what the salt of the *dkhar* looked like. Now you cannot do without it. Look at Lang, what a man he has become. So, tell your father, we'll go after *Ïaïong* has passed. Tell him, I said so."

Just then, Ban, Dorsing's father, came round the corner. He had heard every word. ""Um", he said, "you are not the only one who can talk the language of the *dkhar*. I know their tongue as well as you do.

It is time to part ways especially after what happened last time. If you don't care for my opinion, I might as well disregard yours. I will go when the time suits me, Dorsing, of course, will go with me, so will Lang. As for you, Korbar will always be there to accompany you. Dorsing, it is getting late, let us go home!"

Part Three

CHAPTER ONE
The Storm

Bor could never understand what really happened—it was one of those mysteries that would deepen with the passage of time, a mystery that defied explanation because it happened to him and him alone. No one referred to it. It was something to be mentioned rarely—if at all with a sigh and a beseeching plea to the heavens.

The whole village seemed to share a vague, approximate knowledge about the storm. He had the feeling that they knew something he didn't and it infuriated him. The storm killed his young son, that was all he cared about. He did not care for the gruesome details of how it actually happened. He sat in the doorway of his sister's hut. His niece, Rupa and nephew, Shan, were inside. It was nice to be back in Mawsan, his own village, but he wished it was under different circumstances. He had reluctantly accepted 'Um Ban's hospitality for some time. Now he was with his sister because he wanted to get away from Nonglum for some time.

He sat thinking about the events of the past month. It was so difficult to adjust to the new circumstances. There were so many things he had taken for granted.

The sun was harsh on his eyes. He squinted and saw his wife approaching, trudging slowly with her heavy cane basket. It was a barren landscape offering little to man. He wondered how his brother-in-law managed to coax the earth into producing vegetables.

The woman cried out, "Bahdeng! Where are you?" and then turning to her husband "I thought you had left". She probably expected him to come up with an excuse. Of late, he had shown no willingness to contribute to the general requirements of the household. There was a lot of firewood to be gathered, chopped and stacked. There was a lot of work to be done but he showed no inclination to help.

Bor showed no sign of response, only his big toe wiggled as usual. She remembered how irritating that particular habit was in the early days.

Turning to the right, she put down her cane basket all the while muttering to herself, "What will become of us? Oh God the Maker, the Creator, you who know and see the truth, the injustice of it all. Is it because of some crime we have committed, some taboo we have broken? There is no explanation; I am at a loss to understand! What will become of us?"

The furrows on her face refused to let the sweat trickle down. Her eyes smarted from the fierce heat of the sun and she wondered why her husband spent his days staring into space. Yes, she admitted, it was not easy to ignore the sneers, the barbs. But one had to get on with life and hope that the children coped with it all. The memories of that afternoon remained as vivid as if the events took place yesterday.

It was one of those unpredictable *Ïaïong* days when the bright morning sun would suddenly give way to a furious thunderstorm. They had left early, at the crack of dawn to go to Pandua market. She had taken Bon along with her and with Mother of Neh and other fellow-villagers had looked forward to a day of brisk trade. There were so many things she wanted to buy. She had gone to Mei Krin's stall and the choicest betel leaf was displayed to her. Bon's mother ran her fingers through the tapering ends to check the quality. Satisfied, and after some bargaining deposited the bunch of leaves in her basket. She bartered honey in return for dried fish and also bought huge fish with the cowries Bor had given her. She was conscious of Mother of Neh's envious looks. Why, she rather enjoyed the attention she received from the vendors.

The trade was brisk and lively. Plainsmen vied with each other to engage customers. The tribesmen living in the vicinity had no difficulty in conversing fluently in the language of the *dkhar*. Their brothers from the upland areas were more reticent, unfamiliar with the sights and sounds of Pandua plurality. And so, the hours passed. The clouds gathered and droplets fell on the market-goers. The shopping was soon disrupted by heavy rain. As they returned home in the evening, the conversation was about the purchases they made. Bon and her mother had a considerable load to carry Bor, of course, had his own share. Together, they all made their way slowly, up the gentle slopes. The chatter soon died down as they reached the steep cliffs. There were traces of a storm that had left a destructive trail along its path. Broken twigs and branches were everywhere, the streams were red and muddy and the waters flowed fast sweeping everything along their way.

A light drizzle prompted Bor to say, "Aren't we lucky to have escaped the storm? I believe this drizzle will soon stop".

His wife readily agreed. Little did they know that their world had changed drastically. The journey continued, it was growing dark and there was a sense of discomfort as they saw trees twisted and broken by the wind. When they reached the village, they saw evidence of destruction. There was fear and trepidation on the faces of those who came out of their huts to look at them. The men looked at him saying nothing. Finally, his hut came into view. Broken and battered it bore little resemblance to its former self.

Then, they told him, led him by the hand, to the house of 'Um Ban, the nearest relative where his son Bahduh lay dead, crushed by the storm.

Something snapped. Bor got down on his knees and howled, a terrifying sound that silenced all who were present there. The body of his beloved son was inert, lifeless, without motion. His wife soon started screaming hysterically, unable to absorb the shock of it all. "Bahduh, my son, what has happened to you?", she cried.

The fish looked incongruous, a luxurious item that seemed irrelevant. Soon the village folk flocked to the hut to pay their condolences. Messengers were sent far and wide to relatives to inform them of the tragedy. Meanwhile, food was hurriedly prepared for the mourners. Some intrepid neighbours whispered into the weeping mother's ear apparently asking for permission to cook the fish. Mother of Bon nodded, oblivious to such matters. She was, after all, grief-stricken and could think of nothing else.

Later, with a degree of satisfaction, some remarked they had never tasted such fish.

Eight months after the storm, they left their temporary shelter and returned to Nonglum. They built a hut on the outskirts of the village, it was better for their father, Bon's mother said.

CHAPTER TWO
The Aftermath

The winter was rather severe. The chilly mountain wind chapped faces, hands and feet. The sun shone occasionally, but it could be seen rather than felt. Somehow, its warmth could never penetrate enough to touch one's skin. The leaves fluttered in the wind, listlessly resigning themselves to the whims of the breeze as it blew.

Bon wearily gathered the soiled clothes into a bundle, tied a firm knot and put it into the basket which she then slung over her head. There were times when she hated the company of the other women at the village stream. In summer, of course, there was not much of a problem but in winter she had little choice for the stream dried up at many places. She hated the gossip, the conversation that went on. If she was present, invariably the conversation would turn to her and her family. Once it even turned nasty when she could control herself no longer. It all started when she spread her clothes out to dry in the sun. Mother of Neh, once a neighbour and close family friend, remarked that Bon should have given away to poor relatives such torn items of clothing. Since then, Bon had learnt to rein in her reactions.

She walked quickly, hoping to finish early. She wondered, as tears filled her eyes, how it had come to this. Her father, once respected was now a dejected old man, forgotten by society, by the very people who had once knelt before him for a favour. Her mother pretending to be strong, was actually a bundle of nerves—held together by sheer necessity. Bon did not even want to think of her siblings. Her sisters talked about the calamity but she could see the hurt, the pain and the confusion. Her brother Bahdeng was old enough to understand but he never said anything. The sudden transition had left him numb, unable to mouth his feelings. She could see it in his eyes. She wondered what he saw in hers. She longed to reassure him, tell him things he wanted to hear but she knew, deep down that everything had changed.

She thought often of that day, the day that brought about such upheaval and always, always her intuition gnawed at her reason. She knew her uncle had something to do with the disappearance of all the gold ornaments her mother kept in a big wooden box. Reason, however, told her that her uncle's explanation was quite plausible. The cyclonic gust of wind had spiral-like turned and twisted the thatch, the wooden beams were flung into the sky and the household articles were scattered over a large area. The wooden box was never found. Bon recalled the priceless jewellery kept in the box. Her father had brought some from Shilot, and among them the large coral beads were the most beautiful. If only they had the jewellery. Of course, land was no problem and they grew their own food but the climb down was difficult. For a long time they were used to rice. Now they had to make do with tapioca and yam.

Without being aware of the passage of time she reached the spring. Wearily she put down her basket. She was glad to be alone.

CHAPTER THREE
Spring

Two years had passed since Kupar died. Bon was no longer the most sought after bride. Indeed without her usual fine clothes she was as nondescript as any other poor village girl. Her two sisters found suitable young men to marry because they had no high expectations. They adjusted to the changed circumstances and were not choosy about their husbands. But how could she who had been betrothed to the finest young man in the village settle for anyone less. She could not help comparing the other youths to Kupar and she realised that they always fell short. Her nephews and nieces filled the small hut with their crying. They sometimes laughed and frolicked. Bon found no joy in their presence. There were times when she felt they would drive her mad.

Day after day her existence revolved round the fields that adjoined the village. She spent the time tilling the ground planting vegetables and other crops. There were days when she would fiercely attack the soil compelling it to be fruitful. There were days when she felt she no longer had any strength left. Even raising the hoe from the ground was difficult.

And the arguments continued. She was sick of her mother, always complaining, always saying there was not enough of this or that. She wanted to scream, how could there possibly be if all you do is complain instead of working?

She wondered rather curiously what her mother's reaction would be if she really screamed at her. As she straightened her back and looked at the skies, she thought deeply about her family's condition. It was then that she saw him—Lumbor. Not again! she thought.

"Ko Kongthei!, shall I help you?—you seem to have a lot to do", he cried out.

"*Khublei shibun*, but I can manage" she said, muttering to herself. "I can do without your company."

"Huh! What did you say? Shall I come down?" and without waiting for a reply, he jumped down, walked swiftly along the narrow ledges and reached the flat patch of land she was trying to tame.

"You really work hard, don't you? Here, let me help", he took the hoe from her hands and started to dig the earth. Wiping the sweat from her brow she sat down nearby, watching him. It was always the same.

Day after day, he would help her for an hour or two and then leave saying the same thing everyday.

Lumbor did not give up. One afternoon, during spring time when the cool air had pushed the winter chill aside and the green leaves again covered the once dry, naked branches, he finally gave Bon an indication of his intentions. After some particularly hard work, he sat down on a stone nearby and said.

"Kongthei, you know my intentions—they are honourable and just. I do not know what your feelings are, you have given me little encouragement but nevertheless, I have spoken to my parents and my uncle regarding the matter."

Hesitantly, he continued, "I don't know, if your father is keeping well enough to talk about such matters but I suppose your uncle will be the right person",—he stopped and looked at her. She kept quiet, plucking at the grass near her feet.

He went on—"Kongthei, listen to me, my people will pay your family a visit and I do want you to accept me. I am not rich but I can work hard to provide you a secure comfortable life. I know you have had a rough time. Your family has indeed gone through a great deal of suffering. Your sisters, Kerimai and Tiewsien have begun life afresh. Why don't you?" Bon stared at her feet, chapped and covered with dust. She didn't know what to tell him. How could she tell him she was indifferent to the whole thing. Lumbor looked at her and finally said, "Have I been talking to a stone or a lifeless object! Bon, do say something", he pleaded.

She stood up, picked up her hoe and put it in her cane basket. It was the planting season, the earth had to be ready but she decided to call it a day. She began to collect all the other implements and put them in her basket. She could feel Lumbor's eyes on her.

"Look!" he said, "I know how you feel but you have to learn to accept what has happened. Forget the past and try to think of a future that will bring you peace and happiness. You think too much about the past, you know Kongthei, that burden has to be thrown away. Kongthei, look at me"—She turned her head away from him, away from someone who dared to speak her innermost thoughts.

Exasperated, he threw his hands up and told her, "Do not imagine that you are the only person in this world to undergo suffering".

"You see" she said, trying to keep her voice level. "You do not understand nor do I expect you to. Tell me, how would you feel if your family was in the same situation, cursed by fellow villagers, looked upon with a mixture of pity, curiosity and ignored most of the time. Do you think it has been easy for me to watch my father being reduced to a ghost of what he formerly was? Day after day, I have to listen to the laments of our fall from prosperity to poverty. Yes, my sisters have adjusted, somehow they have been able to get on with life but I cannot, I simply cannot just put it all behind me. How can I when I see my parents shattered, absolutely devastated by what has happened?"

Lumbor turned and gazed rather abstractly at the horizon, "Yes, yes, I fully understand, but you see Bon, you have to admit that things happen because of certain reasons. I hope you don't take offence but as everybody in the village says, wealth that comes like the swift muddy torrents of summer disappears as suddenly. Only God the Creator knows the truth and who am I to pass judgement? But I feel for you, I want to make you happy, don't you understand?" He looked into her eyes and smiled. He stood there for some time, and then turned away.

She watched him leave as he climbed the slope but her heart was heavy. She wondered aloud, why couldn't I be like Kerimai and Tiewsien? They went about their daily tasks with a sense of immediacy which she envied. They often talked about the bygone days but they actually lived in the present which they found more absorbing than anything else. Their husbands were equally insensitive to such things, coming as they did from families who knew nothing but their relationship with the earth that sustained them. They were men who spent their days planting, nurturing, harvesting. They bartered the produce, if they could not consume all. The highlight of their existence was the village market day where they could meet, exchange news, bring back some foodstuff and generally feel content with their lot.

Bon existed on a different plane. She participated in all these activities but she did so without involving her soul, her emotions. She had seen it all, a life of plenty, a life of adversity, the thrill of success, the pain of death. What did she profit from it all—now, she knew no one wanted a poor relative, she knew all about fair-weather friends. In some way, she felt a distinct bond connecting her to Bahdeng, her brother who spoke little but showed signs of understanding her predicament.

CHAPTER FOUR
Leaving Home

Yet it happened. Finally she gave in. It was one of those days when the arguments were more heated than usual. Her youngest sister, Tiewsien, and her mother ganged up against her accusing her of a thousand and one things. The implication was that she depended on her sister for everything and contributed little to the general well-being of the family. Fed up, she told them she would leave. "Go where?" they asked her. "I'll marry", she said. Cackles of laughter ensued. "Who would marry you", Kerimai retorted. "You refused Lumbor when his uncle visited last month with a marriage proposal, no one else wants to marry you, moreover you are growing old and there are many young girls in the village".

Angrily, Bon walked out of the hut, startling the chickens in the front yard. She asked herself, had she made a mistake in refusing to marry Lumbor? No, no, it was her uncle. She detested him. She hated the insinuations he made that she had better marry Lumbor because under the circumstances this offer was likely to be the last one. She remembered her uncle's remarks about his daughter's case being different. She was pretty, well-off and every young man in the village had his eyes on her.

Bon had felt so insulted but she had kept quiet. Later, her uncle had remonstrated with her but to no avail. Her mother had joined the chorus and that made her only more determined. Her father had simply sat through the whole thing. He was there yet not there. Suddenly, the urge to get away became stronger and stronger. She wanted to break free. But where can I go? She asked herself.

She went out to the fields and worked hard the whole day. Digging, the thoughts running through her mind, she decided she would go to her aunt's house in Mawsan. Lumbor's house was close by. At noon, Bahdeng came to the fields. She wan't surprised. The next morning she collected her belongings, put them in her basket and to the amazement of her mother and sister, she bid goodbye. At first they stared open-mouthed, then they started laughing, derisively sneering at her, her youngest sister calling out, "So Kongthei, are you going to Lumbor". And Bon cried out, "So what if I am?"

She hoisted the basket up and went to her father who as usual spent his day staring into space. She touched him lightly on the shoulder and said, "Pa, I am going away for some time". She then walked across the sun-baked mud and turned to the right towards the village path across which lay several thick dark green bushes which were still wet with dew.

Her father did not turn his head.

CHAPTER FIVE
The Call of the Plains

Life with Lumbor was peaceful enough. She liked her new environs. She was no stranger to the village of Mawsan, her father's village, but again she felt the difference between her cousins and herself. Shan was rather successful in his trade, eager to adapt and learn the business his uncle had taught him. Rupa had married a fine young man from the same village. Wan and the rest of the brothers were doing well in their own trades. As she nursed her baby boy, Rishan at her breast, she thought of Lumbor. He wasn't bad really, but something made her restless, she was not sure what exactly made her uneasy.

Life went on in fits and starts but she had nothing to complain about. The following year she delivered a baby girl and the children kept her busy. Lumbor tilled the fields, brought the crop home and generally seemed contented with life. He worked hard and Bon began to loosen up somewhat, the vitality and energy she used to have, seemingly making a return.

It was not for long, Lumbor began to show signs of dissatisfaction with his own condition. He grumbled. He talked of Shan and other men of the village who profited from business at Pandua and Shilot. Bon did not like it. She did not like it one bit. It brought back memories and a nagging fear at the back of her mind.

She knew it was coming. It was the fifth year of her marriage. They were to hold the naming ceremony for her daughter and as usual, three suitable names had been tentatively chosen. Her mother and sisters would be coming and she was busy cleaning the floor of the hut. They had long ago shed their differences and accepted her new way of life.

The day arrived and they all sat in the doorway ready for the ceremony. Carefully, the gourd containing home-made brew was tilted to determine the suitability of a name. The droplets clung to the gourd in favour of the name Lisimai and so it was.

Her folk stayed on till market day and then after a few purchases left for their own village. Shortly after, on a fine autumn morning when the butterflies crowded the trees at the edge of the compound and as she was feeding mashed bananas to the little one, Lumbor suddenly said,

"Mother of Rishan, I have been thinking lately, perhaps it is better for us if . . . uh . . . if . . ."

"If what?" interrupted Bon.

"If, you see, Mother of Rishan, I join the trading party of Shan when he leaves in the winter. You have seen Shan and the profit he has been able to make, what do you say? Don't you think it will be better for us, so that we can cater to our needs and requirements."

"What needs?" asked Bon, "have I ever complained? We have enough to get by, what else do you require? Let us not hanker for too much. I am quite contented with what we have. I don't understand you", she said.

The baby began to wail as if sensing the argument between the two.

"No, Mother of Rishan, be reasonable, do not speak out of emotion, look at the facts, look at people you know, almost all have profited from the trade, some have done well, some have small gains, that is according to their fate and destiny. But what is the harm in trying?" Bon tried to calm the child and feed her, all the while thinking about her husband's words. It must have been Shan, she thought, who asked her husband to go along with him.

"I don't know, what can I say?" said Bon. "I do not like your idea. Let us make do with what we have. We will eat our tapioca, our yam, whatever we plant and produce".

Lumbor started to protest, "But why are you so unwilling to let me go? What are you scared of?" And then he began to enumerate men from the same village who were in the business. Bon kept quiet. Lumbor did not understand her. She was sure of that. How could he understand her deepest fears, the old memories that had brought her so much pain and suffering. Deep down, was a fear of failure, disaster brought about by the unhappy experiences of her father. No, she told herself, this was her husband and there was every possibility he would succeed. But the whole idea bothered her. The baby suddenly burped, and vomited the mashed banana all over its chest. Bon hurriedly wiped it off with a rag nearby and realized that in her agitation she had been feeding the baby too much banana.

Lumbor stood up and took his knife and basket and as he turned to go away, said to her, "Well, it's time for me to go to the fields, think about what I have said."

CHAPTER SIX
The Return to Nonglum

It was as she feared. When Lumbor returned from his trip to Shilot, he brought little evidence of the profits he said he would make. She taunted him at night and ridiculed him. She would tell him,

"So, you are my cousin's porter, are you, where is the profit my husband?"

And he would say. "Give me time, give me time, I am learning the business. You cannot expect me to be wealthy overnight. You know, very well, what happens when wealth comes too quickly. It is better that a man becomes wealthy gradually over the years."

She understood the hidden barbs and the arguments continued. Due to his new aspirations he had neglected the fields and crops and so Bon found another reason to find fault with him. She had tried her best to manage in his absence but it was of little use.

The following year, she was back in her own village. She could not take it any more. She remembered that it was raining when she left him. The heavens had opened up and the rain poured down in continuous streams. As she stepped out of the hut, she remembered Lumbor saying,

"Come back! you stupid woman, you will kill the children".

She had continued walking, carrying the little one on her back, Rishan following her, terrified. She looked back and saw her husband still gesticulating and apparently shouting but all she heard was the sound of the rain.

In retrospect, it would have been funny to leave Lumbor on a bright and sunny day. It would not have been proper. There was laughter when she left home six years ago but when she returned home with the children straggling behind her, tired and wet, there was only silence.

Her father sat in the same place, it was as if he had not moved for six years. Only, the thin bony hands with their prominent knuckles reflected the passage of time.

Bon was not worried about the children. They had never known anything but poverty; they would like their new home. The children soon scampered about with their cousins though they did find their grandfather a little strange. He seldom spoke and sat outside the hut the whole day, staring straight ahead, sometimes dropping off to sleep. Her mother had aged. Sadness and sorrow had taken their toll. She pottered around but her back was bent with too much work and her complaints were endless. She soon learnt from her mother that her uncle seldom visited them and when he did he never stopped reminding them about their misfortune. Bon fumed inside but there was little she could do.

Kerimai and Tiewsien questioned her about her husband but her curt replies soon silenced them. After some days, they soon settled to a new routine. Kerimai, of course, lived in a small hut a little further down the hill. Tiewsien, the youngest was responsible for the parents and also her now destitute elder sister. Bon helped in the fields all day. Her brother-in-law was hardworking and Bon soon learned to fit in.

At night, she told stories to her children but they missed their father's songs. If there was anything Lumbor was good at, it was singing and playing the *duitara*. At night he would take the instrument and tell them stories of the big rock that swallowed human beings. He would begin by saying,

"In the days of yore, when animals and birds spoke with man . . . ." And he would continue weaving tales of legends, of battles fought between villages, of myth and magic and make characters come alive through his songs.

Bon sang lullabies and tried to make up for Lumbor's absence but one night, her daughter said rather churlishly,

"I like father's singing. I want to go back to father."

Bon was speechless. She tried to pacify Lisimai by saying that father had gone to a far-away place and would soon return.

CHAPTER SEVEN
A Memorable Encounter

The seasons came and went. Nonglum saw births, deaths and marriages. She received news about Lumbor. He was not doing too badly still accompanying Shan whenever he went to the plains. Lumbor's uncle had come once to Nonglum to ascertain the facts about her separation from Lumbor. She had to admit that she sounded foolish as she tried to explain her stand to the old man. The fact was, she could not give a satisfactory explanation and the old man left expressing hope that since Lumbor did not seem inclined to take a new wife it would be in the best of things if Bon returned to her husband's village. Bon simply nodded. She would take her time.

Bon never went to marriages. She was too conscious of her own appearance and the tattered clothes. She sent her children though; she did not want them to be isolated. She seldom went to Pandua market, it was no joy to watch others spend.

One *Ïaïong* morning, however, she left reluctantly with Tiewsien and brother-in-law to go to the market.

Every year, the month of *Ïaïong* reminded her of her brother's death. As they left the village, she told her sister,

"You remember, don't you, it was on a day such as this when Bahduh died."

Her sister replied in the affirmative. Soon they talked about other things as they were joined by fellow-villagers.

At the market, Bon followed her sister around somewhat tired after the journey. As she watched the different stalls, she suddenly noticed a crowd in a section of the market. She pressed closer to the crowd looking intently at the man who was the object of all the attention. She couldn't hear him properly, couldn't understand him. A young man was standing next to her craning his neck eagerly.

"What is the man saying?" she asked the man.

"Oh! He's talking about a man called Jesus, who can forgive sins and set you free!"

"Set you free from what?", she asked, confused.

"Set you free from the past, from sins".

That's new, she thought. "What else is he saying?", she asked.

"Something about casting your burden on this new God, and he will give you rest. What rubbish!", remarked the young man.

She watched in wonder! She did not understand much of what was said but she found it strange that so many people were listening to him. Looking around, she found many others carrying on with their business of buying and selling. The speaker went on and on, his voice at times raised and loud, to make a point, at other times, soft and pleading. She continued to stand there half-ashamed to be listening to the man. After a few minutes, she walked away somewhat conscious of herself.

As she turned to walk away, she saw the fish-vendors right across her. There were fresh big *khathli* and her mouth watered. Tentatively, she walked towards the array of fish in the shallow cane baskets.

"Can I have that fish, please?" she timidly asked the vendor. He looked at her and saw the cowries on her outstretched palm.

"Oh! I'm sorry", he said, "I can give you this"— he held up a small fish. She took it quickly and put it in her basket.

The journey home was a tedious one for Bon. They asked after her father and she felt uncomfortable talking about him. She met her uncle and cousin, Dorsing and noted their air of well-being and prosperity. Most of all, she was surprised to learn that there were some tribesmen who had accepted the "new faith". At first she did not know what the others were referring to.

"What new faith?" she questioned and they asked her if she had seen the man talking in the market place. And then she understood.

She forgot all about it when she reached home. Her father was ill, unable to move. The problem with him was he talked very little, no one could really understand his illness. He was thin and pale, his tall frame, a mere skeleton. He complained that his head was aching but no amount of massage or herbal compress could bring him relief. He saw things and he saw people, crying out sometimes to unseen persons. He lived in a world they knew nothing about.

Chapter Eight
The Return of Summer

In the deep recesses of his memory, Bor saw other things, other people—an old woman dying, whispering with her last breath. "You have deprived me of my rightful share, Bor, you will get what is due to you."

He remembered how he protested, not knowing the end was so near—but the life went out of her soon after. She never heard his plea of innocence. Did I wrong her? It was a matter he had long forgotten or pretended to. Now he recalled his aunt and like a flash the past passed before his eyes.

It was a summer day. He got up from the floor where he had been lying. The hut was quiet, his daughter was nowhere to be seen, and his small grandchildren were outside. He wanted to get away from memories, from people. He understood them no longer. Mechanically his feet took him forward. He saw no one. He met no one.

The rain clouds were gathering, and the fog was creeping over the mountain slopes. It was chilly, the whiteness grasping and clinging to his body. It had been raining for many days; there was dampness all around. He shivered, his tattered clothes providing little relief. His steps were heavy, he walked towards the cliff top located a short distance from his hut. He was amazed at his own strength. But he was soon exhausted. Halfway he stopped, panting, gasping for breath. Slowly he made his way struggling to reach the top. It was difficult; he dragged his feet, forcing them to obey his will. Finally, he stood there.

He could not see much through the fog, the drizzle coated his hair and still he stood there listening to the roar of the waterfall. They were familiar sounds, dearer to him than people. Eagerly he stepped forward towards the edge of the rock to bathe himself completely in the sound of the roaring cataract. The thick fog swirled, rose from the gorge and covered him entirely. For a few seconds the man became a blur—a strong gust of wind, a stone displaced tumbling into the gray, gaping unfathomable nothingness below and the next moment when the fog lifted—he was no longer there.

Bon watched the water dripping from the eaves, thinking wondering when they would find him. The nightmare would never vanish from her memory. They looked for him in hill and valley. She knew they grumbled, she heard them sometimes when they came back from the search. She felt the burden on her shoulders. "It is too heavy for me to bear", she muttered to herself. And then as she waited for news, she remembered the speaker at Pandua market. Was that promise real?

Six days later, when the rain lessened somewhat, they finally found him. The body was lying on a narrow ledge, caught among some bushes, bruised and broken. When they brought his body home on a bamboo bier she did not cry. Her tears were already spent. It was different with her mother. She promptly collapsed. When she woke up, her cries rent the air as she wailed and moaned and extolled the virtues of a man no one could understand.

There were people everywhere. They crowded the hut and the body lay outside. Bon sat beside the body. She heard snippets of conversation; she was not sure whether they were meant for her ears,

"jumped over the cliff."

"no! no! was mad, not in his senses."

"of course, such an unnatural death,—should not be kept inside."

"does not augur well for the family . . . ."

Bon realized there were so many things that needed to be done.

A village near Sohra. Unusual. It was the rainy season but it did not rain that day. In the mountains nearby the mists were rising from the deep gorges and the waterfalls thundered their way down the steep cliffs to dissolve in a rainbow and a smoky pool at the foot.

EPILOGUE

The Sumos snaked their way along the serpentine road. They were carrying hordes of garrulous tourists eager to see Cherrapunjee the wettest place on earth. Alighting at several vantage points, they marched up and down capturing the stunning scenery with their cameras.

The guide pointed out the falls, took them to the cave and recited well-worn descriptions. He knew it all by heart. But he did not like questions. He could always smell the academic types with their endless curiosity and obsession with dates. He remembered that in the early days as a very young man, he was never quite sure about the difference between stalactites and stalagmites. With a grandiose sweep of his arm he used to say "and these, ladies and gentlemen are the stalactites and the stalagmites." Now he knew better.

After exhausting the God-made spectacular sights he would take them to the man-made park on the other side. Not everything was artificial, though. From a specially constructed viewpoint the vast plains of Bangladesh could be seen. It was summer and there was water everywhere.

And the tourists from Bangladesh marvelled at the sight. In the mountains nearby the mists were rising from the deep gorges and the waterfalls thundered their way down the steep cliffs to dissolve in a rainbow and a smoky pool at the foot.